WHEN I WAS YOUNG IN THE MOUNTAINS

WHEN I WAS YOUNG IN THE MOUNTAINS

by Cynthia Rylant

illustrated by Diane Goode

E. P. DUTTON · NEW YORK

Library of Congress Cataloging in Publication Data

Rylant, Cynthia.   When I was young in the mountains.

Summary: Reminiscences of the pleasures of life in the
mountains as a child.
[1. Mountain life—Fiction.   2. United States—Social life
and customs—20th century—Fiction] I. Goode, Diane, ill.
II. Title.
PZ7.R982Wh   1981   [E]   81-5359
AACR2

Published in the United States by E. P. Dutton,
a division of NAL Penguin Inc.,
2 Park Avenue, New York, N.Y. 10016

Editor: Ann Durell   Designer: Riki Levinson

W   15 14 13 12 11 10 9

for my grandparents, Elda and Ferrell Rylant
C. R.

for Nicole and Christopher Capuozzo
D. G.

When I was young in the mountains, Grandfather came home in the evening covered with the black dust of a coal mine. Only his lips were clean, and he used them to kiss the top of my head.

When I was young in the mountains,
Grandmother spread the table with hot
corn bread, pinto beans and fried okra.

Later, in the middle of the night,
she walked through the grass with me to the
johnny-house and held my hand in the dark.
I promised never to eat more than one serving
of okra again.

When I was young in the mountains,
we walked across the cow pasture and through
the woods, carrying our towels. The swimming
hole was dark and muddy, and we sometimes
saw snakes, but we jumped in anyway.

On our way home, we stopped at
Mr. Crawford's for a mound of white butter.
Mr. Crawford and Mrs. Crawford looked
alike and always smelled of sweet milk.

When I was young in the mountains,
we pumped pails of water from the well at
the bottom of the hill, and heated the water
to fill round tin tubs for our baths.

Afterward we stood in front of the
old black stove, shivering and giggling,
while Grandmother heated cocoa on top.

When I was young in the mountains,
we went to church in the schoolhouse
on Sundays, and sometimes walked with the
congregation through the cow pasture
to the dark swimming hole, for baptisms.

My cousin Peter was laid back into the
water, and his white shirt stuck to him,
and my Grandmother cried.

When I was young in the mountains,
we listened to frogs sing at dusk and awoke
to cowbells outside our windows. Sometimes
a black snake came in the yard, and my
Grandmother would threaten it with a hoe.

If it did not leave, she used the hoe
to kill it. Four of us once draped a very
long snake, dead of course, across our necks
for a photograph.

When I was young in the mountains,
we sat on the porch swing in the evenings,
and Grandfather sharpened my pencils with his
pocketknife. Grandmother sometimes shelled
beans and sometimes braided my hair. The dogs
lay around us, and the stars sparkled in the sky.
A bobwhite whistled in the forest.
Bob-bob-bobwhite!

When I was young in the mountains,
I never wanted to go to the ocean, and I never
wanted to go to the desert. I never wanted
to go anywhere else in the world, for I was
in the mountains. And that was always enough.